This book **belongs** to

.........................................................

Written by Alexander Cox.
Illustrated by Clare Fennell.

Inspired by an idea from Andrea Bennett.

# Mince Pie Mice

**Alexander Cox ★ Clare Fennell**

make
believe
ideas

'Twas the night before Christmas,
when all through the house
**not** a creature was stirring . . .

. . . not even a **mouse.**

**What?**
Not even a **mouse?**
Don't be so **naïve.**

How could we **sleep** all **night?**
**Mice** love **Christmas Eve!**

My name's Basil!

NO FLYING

I'm WHISKERS!

And that over there is Bryce.

Let us show you why it's **great** being

christmas mice.

We'll **start** with . . .

**FOOD!** Glorious food.
There for us to **take!**

Chocolates, CANDIES, cookies, and grand gingerbread bakes!

With **veggies**, **meats**, and CHEESE galore
(no **human** will want to **touch**).

Christmas isn't just for food.
There's way more to explore!
Your house is a mouse funfair,
decked up from roof to floor.

We zipline down from fairytop
dangling by our tails!

Inside your tree, we put on **plays**
with a **merry festive twist.**

Then it's time for the big **dance**
no **rodent** can **resist!**

But don't be fooled by all the fun: tonight is **hard work** too.

Hickory-dock! Look at the clock!

Our **special guest** is due.

**Important** jobs? You may ask. What is there to do?

Here's a **Christmas secret** that no one has told you.

Santa Claus is just one man
with lots of **jobs** tonight.

He needs a **helping hand** to make each Christmas a **delight!**

What about his **team of elves?**
I can **hear** you cry.

Well, they make the **toys** and **gifts**,
but they **don't like** to **fly!**

So, each **house** has mice like us,

no matter the **address.**

We're the **secret key** to making Christmas a **success!**

We **wrap** the **gifts**

and **write** the **tags**

and **tie** the **pretty bows.**

Then place them all **beneath** the tree
in **neat** and **tidy** rows.

We **sweep**, we **clean**, we **decorate**,
and finish your **surprise.**

Then **Santa** lets us nibble on
some **CARROTS** and **mince pies!**

Think of all the joy she'll bring
each special Christmas Day.

That's it for another year.
Time to vanish out of sight.

Happy Christ-mice to all

and to all a good-night!